HAPPY Birthday imagination

Happy birthday, Puffin!

Did you know that in 1940 the very first Puffin story book (about a man with broomstick arms called Worzel Gummidge) was published? That's 70 years ago! Since then the little Puffin logo has become one of the most recognized book brands in the world and Puffin has established its place in the hearts of millions.

And in 2010 we are celebrating 70 spectacular years of Puffin and its books! Pocket Money Puffins is a brand-new collection from your favourite authors at a pocket-money price – in a perfect pocket size. We hope you enjoy these exciting stories and we hope you'll join us in celebrating the very best books for children. We may be 70 years old (sounds ancient, doesn't it?) but Puffin has never been so lively and fun.

There really IS a Puffin book for everyone
– discover yours today.

Tom Palmer is a football fan and author. He writes two series for Puffin: Football Academy and Foul Play. He visits schools and libraries every week to talk about reading, writing and football.

It was reading about football that helped Tom to become a confident reader. He now has the job of his dreams: travelling the world to watch football matches, meeting players, then writing stories about them.

He lives in Yorkshire where he likes to be with his family, watch football and run.

You can find out more about Tom – and talk to him – through his website *www.tompalmer.co.uk*

Books by Tom Palmer

Football Academy series:
BOYS UNITED
STRIKING OUT
THE REAL THING
READING THE GAME
FREE KICK
CAPTAIN FANTASTIC

Foul Play series (for older readers):
FOUL PLAY
DEAD BALL
OFF SIDE

TOM
PALMER

THE SECRET FOOTBALL CLUB

Illustrated by
Brian Williamson

PUFFIN

PUFFIN BOOKS

Published by the Penguin Group
Penguin Books Ltd, 80 Strand, London WC2R ORL, England
Penguin Group (USA) Inc., 375 Hudson Street, New York, New York 10014, USA
Penguin Group (Canada), 90 Eglinton Avenue East, Suite 700, Toronto, Ontario, Canada M4P 2Y3
(a division of Pearson Penguin Canada Inc.)
Penguin Ireland, 25 St Stephen's Green, Dublin 2, Ireland (a division of Penguin Books Ltd)
Penguin Group (Australia), 250 Camberwell Road, Camberwell, Victoria 3124, Australia
(a division of Pearson Australia Group Pty Ltd)
Penguin Books India Pvt Ltd, 11 Community Centre, Panchsheel Park, New Delhi – 110 017, India
Penguin Group (NZ), 67 Apollo Drive, Rosedale, North Shore 0632, New Zealand
(a division of Pearson New Zealand Ltd)
Penguin Books (South Africa) (Pty) Ltd, 24 Sturdee Avenue, Rosebank,
Johannesburg 2196, South Africa

Penguin Books Ltd, Registered Offices: 80 Strand, London WC2R ORL, England

puffinbooks.com

First published 2010
1

Text copyright © Tom Palmer, 2010
Illustrations copyright © Brian Williamson, 2010
Colour Puffin artwork on cover copyright © Jill McDonald, 1974
All rights reserved

The moral right of the author and illustrators has been asserted

Set in Adobe Caslon 13.25/25.75 pt
Typeset by Ellipsis Books Limited, Glasgow
Made and printed in England by Clays Ltd, St Ives plc

British Library Cataloguing in Publication Data
A CIP catalogue record for this book is available from the British Library

ISBN: 978-0-141-32820-1

www.greenpenguin.co.uk

Penguin Books is committed to a sustainable future
for our business, our readers and our planet.
The book in your hands is made from paper
certified by the Forest Stewardship Council.

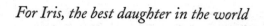

For Iris, the best daughter in the world

Contents

The Railway Children

It was the first day back at school after the summer break. Six weeks of fun and holidays over. Finished.

But Lily, Zack and Khal were not sad to be back – they were delighted. Standing in the playground, they looked around the school grounds. Nothing had changed. Kingsfolly Primary School was as it always had been.

The school building was old and brown. The car park, tightly packed with teachers' cars. The small wood beyond the playground, mysterious as ever. And the playground itself, marked out as a football pitch, ready for the first game of term.

'Kick-off at morning break?' Lily said.

Zack and Khal nodded. Zack was short and stocky with tightly plaited dark hair. He was known for being clever and full of good ideas. Khal was tall and had a thin face.

'Yeah,' Khal said. 'I can't wait.'

'Nor me,' Zack agreed.

'It's been a long time since we've played football,' Lily added, pushing her curly blonde hair away from her face.

And it had been. A very long time.

Kingsfolly Primary School was in the middle of

the city. Its triangular grounds were surrounded by a very busy road on one side and several railway tracks on the other two. Trains thundered loudly past the school every few minutes.

The part of the city where Lily and the others lived was so built up that there was no room for fields and parks. No room for football. There were just houses and shops and warehouses and roads and railways. All packed in together.

The only place children *could* play football, without being flattened by trains and cars, was the school playground.

And that was why they were so excited about being back at school: they hadn't played a proper game of football for weeks. Every time they'd passed Kingsfolly Primary in the holidays they'd gazed longingly at the playground, but there was no way they could get over the four-metre fence that protected it from the outside world.

Zack rubbed his hands together, grinning. 'Did you see that Porsche in the car park?'

'No,' Khal replied. 'Is there really one?'

'*I* saw it,' a voice said above the racket of shouting and screaming in the playground. It belonged to a girl who was now standing next to Lily. She had long dark dreadlocked hair, held back with a tie. Maddie was Lily's best friend. 'It's a Carrera 911,' she added matter-of-factly.

Lily turned to Maddie. 'Do you reckon it's his?'

'Whose?' Zack asked.

'His!' Lily said. 'The new head teacher. Mr Whatsisname.'

'Edwards,' Maddie said. 'Has anyone seen him?'

Everyone shook their head.

'Well, he must be cool if he's got a Porsche,' Khal said, just as the school bell went off.

'We'll find out in assembly,' Lily said, looking at her watch. 'It starts in five minutes.'

And the four friends headed into the school, where they'd find out just how cool their new head teacher really was.

Double Trouble

'Good morning, children.'

'Good-mor-ning-mis-ter-ed-wards,' a hundred and twenty voices chanted back.

Mr Edwards nodded and gazed around the school hall. At the murals on the walls. At the

wooden flooring that gleamed after a polishing. He was a short bald man, wearing a thick black suit and glasses. Watching him, Lily noticed that he had not yet smiled. She remembered the previous head teacher, Mrs Warner, had always smiled.

Lily elbowed Zack. 'Ask him,' she said, grinning.

'What?' Zack said, confused.

'If it's his car. The Porsche.'

Zack shook his head and looked down as he felt Mr Edwards' eyes flick towards him. Then the new head teacher stared at all the children.

'Before we sing,' he said, 'a few announcements.'

Lily looked around at the rest of the children

and teachers. There was *something* strange about the atmosphere today. Something different from how it had been last term. But what was it? And why?

'Firstly, thank you for your welcome this morning,' Mr Edwards said. 'I am very happy to be your new head teacher.'

Lily thought his voice sounded like he didn't mean he was happy at all. It was hard and unfeeling.

'Secondly, I want to let you know that the school celebrates its hundredth birthday in October. And the school's longest-serving teacher, Mrs Baker, has been charged with thinking up a way to celebrate this. I'd like you all to support her as much as you can.'

Lily looked at Mrs Baker, who was their class teacher this year. She was nice. All the children liked her. But Mrs Baker wasn't smiling, even though she'd been mentioned and everyone was looking at her. Lily felt a panic rising in her chest. Something was wrong. She could sense it.

'Thirdly –' Mr Edwards's voice suddenly sounded even harder – 'and before we sing our first song, I need to inform pupils that after a series of injuries in the playground last year and the concern of some parents . . . from now on football and all other ball games are banned in the school grounds.'

There was a huge collective gasp, then silence.

As if everyone had been breathing in, shocked. This news was so sudden. So unexpected.

'I am,' Mr Edwards said, pausing briefly, 'sorry about this. But I have a duty of care to protect you from dangerous activities and the serious injuries you could suffer playing football.'

Lily felt her head go hot inside. And then she realized that she was on her feet. The only child out of all the school.

Mr Edwards looked over his glasses at her. 'Yes?'

'You can't,' Lily said in a whisper.

'I can,' the head teacher said. 'And I will.'

Then Lily felt a hand on her shoulder. It was Mrs Baker.

'Sit down, Lily,' she said in a kind, but very firm, voice.

Lily sat. She could feel her eyes beginning to sting. A thick lump in her throat. Her face itching.

Mr Edwards looked at Lily for a second longer. Then, after an uncomfortable silence, he nodded to Mr Nokes on the piano.

'Now for our first song,' he said, as music filled the hall and everyone stood to sing.

Dead Ball

At morning break Lily, Maddie, Zack and Khal gathered at the far edge of the playground where the small wood stretched to the back of the school grounds. The circle of friends was joined by James and Batts. The six of them had planned to meet here to play football. But that wasn't going to happen. Not now.

Lily eyed James as he came over. He had blond hair and was the tallest boy in Year Six. Lily liked him, even though he was always looking for an argument – and always with her. She hoped they could be on the same side with this.

No football. No football for the rest of the year. No football ever. She couldn't imagine living in a world like that.

'What are we gonna do?' Batts said. 'This is stupid . . . it's . . .' He fell silent.

Lily shrugged, looking at Batts. He was big for a Year Six too. And his hair was always ultra-short.

'She's still upset,' Maddie said to Batts and James, looking at her friend.

'*I'm* upset. We're all upset,' James said, looking cross. 'You're not the only one who can be upset.'

Lily shrugged. 'I didn't say I was.'

James frowned and crossed his arms; Lily wondered why he was always so angry.

Then Zack spoke. He'd been gazing into the woods. But now he was looking at his friends. 'We need to stop feeling angry and sad. We need to think of a way of getting football back.'

'Zack's right. We need a plan,' agreed Lily.

James stepped forward. 'Obviously!'

'But what plan?' Khal asked. 'Mr Edwards looks like he's never changed his mind about anything.'

'Well, he's going to change his mind about this,' Maddie said. 'Isn't he, Lily?'

Lily nodded. 'He is. But how?'

'Did Mrs Baker talk to you in assembly?' Zack asked Lily.

'Yes,' Lily said. 'But only to tell me to sit down.'

No one spoke for a few seconds. They were all thinking. Thinking hard.

Most of them were looking into the woods, as if the answer was in there. But it didn't seem to be. Even if it was, they would not be allowed to find it. They were banned from the woods too; that ban had been standing long before Mr Edwards had come along to spoil things.

The woods *were* part of the school grounds, and children used to be allowed in them. Zack's dad had come to the school when he was young and said he remembered playing in them. Climbing trees. Making dens. That sort of thing.

But now they were out of bounds until the school could raise the money to clear the ground to make them safe. Nobody ever went in the woods. Well, almost nobody.

Still thinking, Lily noticed that Zack was staring at her.

'What?' she said.

'Maybe she's the answer.'

'Who?' Lily tried to figure out what he was talking about. Their teacher? And then she twigged. 'Mrs Baker – that's it! She'll help us! She'll tell Mr *Dead*wards where to go! She's not afraid of anyone.'

Once the others had stopped laughing at Lily's nickname for the new head teacher, they all began to nod.

'That's it,' Khal said.

'Do it,' Batts said.

James just shrugged when Lily looked at him.

'Who's coming with me, then?' she said.

Only Maddie stepped forward. But Lily knew that she had all of them with her as she walked across the playground towards their classroom.

Reading the Game

'I'm sorry, girls. I've talked to Mr Edwards about it and I won't ask him again to change his mind.' Mrs Baker looked them in the eye, one by one, as she said no. She was a soft-voiced woman, with fair hair and sparkling eyes.

Lily and Maddie had asked as soon as Mrs Baker returned to the classroom after morning break.

'But, Mrs Baker . . .' Lily said, and then stopped. She realized she was about to cry and she didn't want to do that in front of the class. She felt sad:

she loved football. They all did. When would they ever get to do it again if they weren't allowed to play at school?

Never. That was when!

Lily returned to her seat and shrugged when she saw the others looking at her from their tables. Zack didn't say a word as she sat down next to him. Maddie was equally silent as she went back to her table.

'Now, Year Six, today we're going to be talking about . . . history!' Mrs Baker said.

Lily watched Khal and Maddie groan. Then she glanced across at Oliver Sykes who had suddenly sat up and looked eager, like a dog expecting a biscuit.

Typical Oliver, she thought. He was always interested, whatever lesson they were having. Except PE. He was one of those boys who loved schoolwork and hated games – especially football. She didn't know why.

'The history,' Mrs Baker went on, 'of . . . football.'

Lily glanced up. Had she heard Mrs Baker right?

'What?' Khal said in a loud confused voice.

'The history of football, Khalid,' Mrs Baker said.

Lily noticed a grin creeping across Khal's face. Maybe this was going to be a good history lesson.

Then everyone was listening – in silence – to the most unexpected history lesson they'd ever had.

'Football used to be played *not* on pitches – *nor* in playgrounds – but across fields and ditches and hedges,' Mrs Baker told them. 'Hundreds of years ago, in the fourteenth century, it was played village against village. The matches would last all day in some cases. And lots of people from each village would play, sometimes hundreds. They played with specially decorated balls. They did it to celebrate their village at certain times of the year.'

Lily was listening with a frown on her face. What was this all about? She looked at Zack. He looked back at her, frowning too.

Their teacher went on to explain that in the olden days the game was called 'mob football' or 'folk football', but it had got so violent that people had broken legs and arms – and had even died – playing it.

'And in 1314 it was banned,' Mrs Baker said, stopping.

The room was quiet. Mrs Baker looked at the children as if she wanted them to say something. But no one did. So she continued: 'King Edward II banned it because he thought it was too dangerous. There were other reasons, but that was the main one.'

'It's like Mr Edwards here,' James muttered.

'What other reasons?' Oliver asked.

Mrs Baker paused, and then said, 'Well, one reason was he wanted his people practising archery, not football. For all the wars they used to fight then.'

'So did they stop playing?' Batts asked.

'Good question,' Mrs Baker replied. 'What do you think?'

'I suppose if the King said they couldn't play, then they didn't play,' Oliver said.

Mrs Baker shook her head. 'No. Even with the threat of prison, they carried on playing.' Then she paused again and looked at her class. Again, no one filled the silence.

'Now, can you remember what Mr Edwards said in assembly?' Mrs Baker asked.

No one spoke. Then Oliver did, smiling. 'That football in the playground is banned.'

'Thank you, Oliver.' Mrs Baker smiled too. 'But not *that*. What did he say about the school's hundredth birthday?'

'That we need to celebrate it?' Maddie said.

Lily looked down at her exercise book. The subject had gone off football and she was sad again.

'And that I am to plan the activities we do,' Mrs Baker said.

No one responded.

'Well, I suggest that each class celebrates by dressing in the clothes of a different century. What do you think?'

'Great!' Oliver said.

'And *you*,' the teacher went on, 'could dress up as people from the . . . fourteenth century.'

Lily stared at the table. Why was Mrs Baker so bothered about dressing up in silly costumes? And what had the fourteenth century got to do with anything? It was *football* that was important.

Journey to the Centre of the Earth

'What was Mrs Baker on about?' Maddie said at lunchtime when they were gathered at their usual place at the far edge of the playground.

Lily shrugged and looked at Zack and Khal, then at James and Batts.

'I'm not sure,' Zack said. 'But I think it was about *something*.'

They stared into the woods. The noise from the playground was as loud as usual. Younger kids running around, chasing each other, older ones standing in groups. Not a ball in sight.

'Let's go in,' Khal said.

'Do we dare?' Lily asked, looking around for one of the teachers on duty.

'I don't think we should,' Maddie contributed.

'I dare,' James said.

'So do I,' Lily said.

'No you don't,' James retorted.

'I do.'

'Prove it.'

Last year, before the summer holidays, they *had* dared to enter the woods. They'd sneaked in and built a den. Just the six of them.

'But Mr Edwards won't like it, will he?' Maddie said, looking at Lily.

'So what? He's not the king, is he?' James said. 'And he never said we couldn't go into the woods. Maybe that rule has been forgotten.'

'Come on,' Batts said.

And, without speaking, one by one, the six children walked along the side of the old sheds and slipped into the woods. They moved through the trees and hanging ivy, over what they thought was an old tennis court that was now overgrown, the court crumbling with weeds and brambles bursting through its surface.

They found their den. A shack they'd built with huge pieces of corrugated iron and sheets of plastic they'd found in the woods. It was unchanged. No one had been in it. Nothing had been moved. The children sat in a circle. Quiet.

'What are we going to do?' Lily asked, breaking the silence. 'About football.'

'Nothing,' James said. 'We can't do anything.'

'We have to,' Khal said.

'But what?' Maddie moaned. 'There's nowhere we can play. Not round where any of us live. And now not in school. We'll never be able to play football again. In our lives.'

'Well, what if Mrs Baker was trying to tell us something?' Zack said.

Lily looked at Zack. If anyone was going to solve their problem, it was him. Zack was clever. He was always the first to find solutions.

'But *what*?' Maddie said again.

'That if it was OK to carry on playing football when it was banned in the fourteenth century,' Zack said, 'then maybe it is now. That Mr Edwards is just a stupid king.'

'She didn't say that,' James cut in.

'But maybe that's what she *meant*,' Lily said, agreeing with Zack.

'So how are you going to play football?' James went on, scowling at Lily. 'It's not like you can put up a massive screen in front of Mr Edwards' office so we can play in the playground. There's nowhere to play. Not for miles.'

No one spoke. James was right.

Lily looked at her watch. She felt sad again. 'We have to go back. Before the end of lunch.'

The six friends stood and ducked out of their den. Lily waited until James was up ahead; he was irritating her. Then they all walked carefully across the old tennis court, trying not to get their legs caught in the tangle of ivy and brambles.

James, Maddie, Khal, Batts and Lily were almost out of the woods when they realized Zack wasn't with them.

'Where's Zack?' Lily asked.

No one knew. They were worried, all thinking the same thing. That he'd fallen. That he was injured or worse. *And* that they'd left him there.

Lily led them back. When they reached the clearing where the old tennis court used to be, they saw Zack. He was standing in the middle of the tennis court, great clumps of ivy and roots in his hands. Lily and Maddie looked at each other, while James frowned and put his hands on his hips.

Then Zack spoke. 'This is it. This is where we can play football. Hidden by a screen . . . of trees!'

Dirty Beasts

For the next two weeks the six children worked tirelessly.

Every break.

Every lunchtime.

Because Zack had had a brilliant idea. The old tennis court: it was perfect for a football pitch. A *secret* football pitch.

Although the surface of the court had been punctured by roots and was strewn with ivy and other plants, it was still a flat surface, as big as a five-a-side pitch. And the best thing was, it was hidden from the school by the dozens of trees that made up Kingsfolly Wood.

Zack had worked out a system. Each break and lunchtime, four of them would go into the woods and clear the court. The other two would act as look-outs: one stood by the old sheds, guarding their entrance to the woods; the other watched the school buildings – including Mr Edwards' office window, which had a view over the woods.

That was how they would protect the Secret Football Club.

Clearing the court was hard. Both hard *work* and also hard not to get filthy moving plants and soil around. During the first couple of days they had smuggled in garden tools from their parents' houses: trowels, the only digging implements small enough to hide in their school bags. They dug and slashed and chopped and hacked.

By Friday of the first week the tennis court looked no different. Except there were huge piles of dead plants and wood at the edge.

'This'll take all year,' Maddie said to Lily.

'Maybe all term?' Lily smiled back at her friend. 'But it'll be worth it. Imagine having our own secret football pitch.'

So they kept at it.

One thing they were careful about was avoiding getting dirty. On the first day Batts was covered in mud. His hands and forearms were filthy, his clothes too. But Zack quickly devised a system to fix that problem.

First, everyone brought in spare clothes to put over their school uniforms as they were clearing the tennis court. Second, whoever was guarding the entrance to the wood had to inspect each of the four clearers on their way out to check if they were dirty. And then the clearers would have to wash their hands at the outdoor tap that was conveniently placed at the back of the old sheds. Because if they were seen to be dirty – or with torn clothes – the teachers would suspect something was going on.

It was hard going, but towards the middle of

the second week things changed dramatically.
Suddenly the tennis court was clear. They could see
how big it was. Now – rather than clearing away
weeds and roots – they were levelling off the pitch
and bringing in soil and small stones from deeper in
the woods to fill holes in its surface. One day it
rained and they used it to their advantage, pressing
mud into the cracks that the ivy had torn up.

*

On the second Friday of term, before they got ready for another round of clearing, Khal was getting impatient. He stood on the lower roots of a tree, looking at the pitch.

'Let's play this afternoon break,' he said. 'It's ready.'

'Not yet,' James said. 'It's not perfect.'

For once Lily agreed with James. 'We need to level off the bottom end first,' she said. 'James is right.'

Khal started climbing the tree. 'It's level. I can see it from here. From above.' He climbed higher.

'It's not level,' Zack said. 'One more day and it'll be right.'

They all gazed down the pitch. It was good. But not perfect.

And as they gazed, away from Khal, away from the tree he was climbing, they heard the noise. A violent crack that echoed around Kingsfolly Wood.

When they looked round, they saw Khal lying on the ground, his eyes closed, and a large branch on top of him.

Don't Tell the Teacher

Once Khal's eyes had opened, James took over.

First, he talked to Khal to make sure he was OK. Then he checked all of Khal's limbs, looking for breaks and deep cuts. The other four crowded round him. The only thing James could find wrong was a rip in Khal's school trousers and a nasty cut on his shin, below his knee.

'You need to get that cleaned up and dressed,' James said.

'It'll be OK,' Khal said, wincing as he straightened his leg.

'Listen to James,' Lily said. 'It could go bad.'

James nodded.

'How do you know about all this, James?' Maddie asked.

'Scouts. We did a first-aid course.'

'Right,' she said, looking impressed.

They helped Khal across the playground. And, as they did, all the other children in school stopped to stare, forming a pathway between the woods and the main door.

All the way Lily was worrying. She could see

teachers' faces at some of the windows on the second floor. And Oliver Sykes watching them, on his own at the edge of the playground.

To make sure Khal got looked after properly, would they need to reveal their secret? How else could they explain his fall – and how dirty he was? Then there'd be no football ever again. Full stop.

Mrs Baker was the first at the door. 'What's happened?' she asked.

Lily said what they'd agreed to say. 'We were behind the sheds – and Khal fell.'

'Let's see,' Mrs Baker said, looking carefully at Khal. 'Bring him up to sick bay. Can he walk?'

'With some help,' Lily replied, frowning.

So, with Maddie on one side and James on the other, Khal limped up the stairs.

This is going OK, Lily thought. Mrs Baker wasn't asking any more questions, and no other teachers had become involved.

They made it up the short staircase, to the sick bay. Maddie, James and Lily crowded round the doorway, Zack and Batts behind them.

Mrs Baker looked at Khal's leg, then at the others. 'You lot go back to the playground,' she said. 'I'll look after Khal. It's not serious.'

But then Lily jumped as another voice came over hers. A man's voice.

'What is going on? How did this happen?

Why are you all so filthy?' It was Mr Edwards.

'What have you children been doing?' He saw

Khalid and looked suddenly worried. 'Khalid, are

you OK?'

'He's fine, Mr Edwards,' Mrs Baker said,

smiling up at the head teacher.

Mr Edwards looked relieved. Then he said,

'Lily? Were you there?' He stepped closer to Lily and seemed to loom over her.

'Yes,' Lily answered, trying to move backwards.

This was it. This was where she was going to get told off and found out and everything else. It was the end. How else could they explain the soil on their hands? They'd not had a chance to wash since Khal fell.

'It's OK, Mr Edwards,' Mrs Baker broke in, speaking in a calm voice. 'Khal has grazed his knee. A small cut. Lily and the others helped him up and into school. And they've all got a bit dirty in the process.'

Mr Edwards looked doubtful. He frowned at

Lily. And Lily thought he knew. About the tennis court. About the Secret Football Club. About everything.

'What I'm more concerned about is Khal's knee,' Mrs Baker went on. 'Mr Edwards, please can you get me some bandages from the supply cupboard?'

With that, Mr Edwards became Mrs Baker's nurse. And the Secret Football Club *remained* a secret, ready for their first game of the season next Monday.

Off Side

Khal found himself easing back in a soft chair as his classmates were doing maths. He could have gone to maths and coped with the pain coming from his sore shin, but this was nicer. Much nicer. He had a glass of milk, a banana and one of the chocolate biscuits left over from lunch to eat. Why go to maths?

In the next room, Mrs Baker was talking to Mr Edwards. It was a small office, with a desk, a computer and a large pot plant in the corner by the window.

Mr Edwards was pacing up and down. He looked worried.

'Tell me again how it happened,' he asked.

'Khal fell. He just tripped over. It happens every lunchtime to someone.'

Mr Edwards stopped pacing and stood still. 'I know,' he said.

Mrs Baker paused for a moment, looking out of the window. Then she spoke. 'You do get terribly worried when the children are in danger, don't you?'

Mr Edwards sighed. 'Yes,' he admitted.

'What is it?'

'What's what?'

'Why do you get so worried? Children play

games and fall over all the time. It's part of growing up.'

'It's . . . W-well . . .' Mr Edwards was stuttering. 'You're thinking about me banning football on my first day, aren't you?'

Mrs Baker nodded.

'I knew you were against that,' he said calmly, 'but it's for their own good.'

'It's not that I'm against it, Mr Edwards. I will support any of your decisions. I just don't understand why you made *that* decision.'

'I should explain.'

'That would help me,' Mrs Baker said.

'When I was young,' Mr Edwards began.

'Ten. The same age as Lily and Khalid and their friends . . .'

'Yes?'

'. . . I played football all day. I loved football. I was good at it.'

Mrs Baker looked shocked. 'Then why . . . ?'

'Why did I ban football?'

'Yes.'

Mr Edwards breathed in. Mrs Baker could see that he was struggling to explain himself.

'Because,' he said eventually, 'that summer – when I was ten – I was playing football with my best friend, Peter, in some fields near where we lived. And . . .' Mr Edwards swallowed. 'And he tripped on a heap of dumped bricks hidden in some long grass. He fell badly. He hurt his head, and his neck. And . . . he was paralysed. For the rest of his life.'

Mrs Baker nodded, but didn't speak. She had to try hard to stop tears forming in her eyes.

Friendly Matches

On Monday morning Lily got to the playground early.

She was too excited not to be at school. She couldn't wait for morning break. When she came in past the high gates and fences Lily expected to be the first to arrive.

But she wasn't.

James was there, talking to Batts. Maddie was there. With Khal. And Zack. They all turned to grin at her together, and she grinned back. This was it! There was just one more thing to decide.

'Who else do we let play?' Lily asked.

'No one,' James replied quickly.

'Three a side isn't enough,' Maddie said.

James shrugged. 'But we'll never be able to trust anyone to keep quiet.'

Lily realized that everyone was looking at her. 'We need two more,' she said. But she wanted to make sure. She didn't want to fall out with James before the first match. 'You pick them, James.'

James looked rather pleased, especially when everyone agreed. He pulled a thinking face. Then, without any more hesitation, he said, 'Finn and Rebecca.'

Now they only had to wait until morning break

before the Secret Football Club could play the first game.

They picked two teams without wasting any time. Lily, Maddie, Zack and Finn versus James, Batts, Khal and Rebecca.

Lily said quietly, 'I declare the Secret Football Club open!' and they kicked off.

Everything felt perfect. The ball was bouncing nicely off their makeshift surface. The only difficulty was playing in silence. It was something they'd decided, to protect their secret.

Playing in the woods was brilliant. Surrounded by trees heavy with leaves turning a nice orange colour. The smell of earth – and the plants they'd cut – filling the air. The sound of birds sometimes replacing the thunder of express trains.

At the start James's team was on top. With Batts in defence (and playing goalie-when-needed) and with Khal up front, they were the perfect four-a-side team. Khal scored first after a great pass from Rebecca.

But then it changed. Lily and Maddie made sure of that. Once they got going, they were hard to stop.

Lily passed to Maddie. Maddie passed to Lily. Goal one.

Then, once they had the ball back, Lily to

Maddie . . . to Zack . . . to Finn . . . to Maddie and it was two—one.

Lily could see James getting mad now that his team was losing. Normally he would shout at his team, order them about. But he couldn't do that in the woods. They had to be quiet. So he had to go up to his team-mates and tell them – in a normal voice – what to do.

And that left holes in their defence. Allowing Maddie to score again.

Three—one.

'This isn't fair,' James shouted.

'Shhhhhhh,' Lily said.

'No way,' James went on, but more quietly. 'You

can't have Lily *and* Maddie on the same team. They're too good.'

Zack watched as Lily, then Khal, tried to calm James down. He knew James hated losing; he always got upset if things were going against him.

Zack looked up at the slight outline of the school behind the trees, as a train whooshed past on the railway tracks. He hoped another train had been coming by when James had shouted. The last thing they wanted to do was draw attention to their games. They had to be hidden and quiet to get away with it.

And you could never be sure if someone was listening – or not.

The Secret Football Club

That week at the end of September was one of the best Lily and her friends could remember. They weren't just playing football; they were playing *secret football*.

And secret football was something special. Knowing that only eight of them were in on the secret felt good. So was playing under the nose of Mr Edwards.

But they didn't neglect school. They worked hard in the classroom, then worked hard on the pitch. Morning break. Lunchtime. Afternoon break.

The score after the first week was 32–30 to

James's team. Really close – and really exciting.

Mrs Baker was still teaching them about the fourteenth century, and that was what Year Six decided to do as a theme for the school's centenary.

Mrs Baker helped the children design the clothes and Maddie's mum cut out the patterns for rough trousers and tops that might have been worn in the fourteenth century. Then the children had to sew their own trousers and shirts together.

Zack suggested they dress up as mob footballers and re-enact a game. And – to everyone's surprise – Mrs Baker agreed. She said it was history – and, therefore, it was fine.

Lily looked over at Oliver Sykes as she said this.

She could see him frowning. She even felt a bit sorry for Oliver: him hating sport so much.

The game that lunchtime was very one-sided. Lily was determined to get back into the lead. She'd spent all morning firing up her team so they'd hit James's team hard.

And that's what they did. Fifteen minutes into the lunchtime game they were level at 32–32. Fifteen minutes after that it was 36–32 to Lily's side. And Lily had scored them all.

When she scored their thirty-sixth goal she noticed James was red in the face. She knew that it was a bad sign. If James was red in the face something dangerous might be about to happen.

James started shouting at his team. 'Batts! What are you doing? You're supposed to be a defender. And, Khal, you haven't scored all day. You're supposed to be a striker. So strike!'

Lily ran over to James. 'Stop shouting, will you? They'll hear you.'

'I won't!' James said, still shouting. 'It's all very well for you to say "stop shouting", but

you're not getting hammered. You're winning!'

Once James had finished, Zack put his hand up. He was glancing back at the playground.

'I can see two dinner ladies looking in,' he said. 'Hit the ground.'

Everyone fell down on to the pitch. Even James. They knew that they could have been heard arguing. And that – if they had – the Secret Football Club might be in grave danger.

They lay for five minutes. Waiting to see if anyone would come to look for them.

But nobody did. So they all stood up and walked carefully off the pitch, out of the woods, across the playground and into school.

Foul Play

'Before we sing,' Mr Edwards said, 'a few announcements.'

It was assembly on Friday morning.

'Firstly, plans are going well for the school's centenary on the tenth of October. Mrs Baker is coordinating a wonderful series of fancy-dress projects in classes. I am sure it's going to be a memorable day.'

Lily smiled at Zack. She couldn't wait to dress up as a fourteenth-century footballer.

'Secondly,' Mr Edwards continued, 'the chess

team had a great win last night, reaching the final of the city chess challenge. Well done, team.'

Applause crackled round the school hall. And Lily grimaced. She wished she could be soaking up the applause for how well her team was doing against James's. But Mr Edwards knew nothing about that.

'And finally,' Mr Edwards said, his smile slipping, his features sharpening, 'the dinner ladies have made me aware that voices were heard in the woods yesterday.' He paused, then went on. 'I am investigating, but need to say *please* do not go in the woods. They are out of bounds. They are dangerous. And if you see or hear anyone in the woods, please tell a teacher or dinner lady immediately.'

Lily could feel the colour draining from her face. She decided not to look at James, even though she was furious with him. It was his shouting that had led to this.

Her mind was a chaos of thoughts. What did Mr Edwards mean when he said he was investigating? She wanted morning break to come. And soon.

They stood in silence when they gathered at break time. No one wanted to blame James, even though it was his fault.

Lily wanted James to say sorry. Then they would be able to move on. But she knew he wouldn't, and she knew no one else would push him. It was down to her to get them through this.

'I think,' Lily started to speak. 'I think that we should all take the blame for Mr Edwards hearing us in the woods.'

She saw James was eyeing her, as if he thought she was going to turn on him.

'We all need to make sure we don't get angry – and that we don't make each other angry.' Lily looked at the others. Maddie and Zack were smiling at her.

Lily noticed that now everyone was watching

her and James. It felt as if they were somehow leaders and it was up to them if they played or not. Then she saw a smile growing on James's face. So she smiled back at him.

'I agree,' Batts added.

'Me too,' Maddie said.

Lily and James nodded. And the rest of Secret FC cheered.

They would play. They couldn't stop now. They loved it too much. And the problems they had were forgotten.

Once they were playing, Lily felt great. Even though James's team had hit back with three goals, and the gap in the scores was reduced: 36–35. She felt happy because she was doing what she loved. With her friends – and that included James.

The ball came to Lily's feet. A short pass from Zack. She trapped it and looked up. James and Khal were in front of her. Maddie ahead of them. She could see the trees waving in the breeze. A light shower of leaves falling on their football pitch. Then she chipped the ball over the heads of James and Khal. To Maddie.

Maddie turned with the ball and slotted it past Batts.

Goal!

Things were good again. For now.

Gathering Storm

Mr Edwards was staring out of his office window. Thinking. He'd been at the school for five weeks now and he felt he was on top of things. He had shown he was in charge. And that was important.

He glanced at his Porsche in the car park. It was safe, he knew. But he always had to check.

He liked the school. He was happy. Even though there were cars and trains and buildings everywhere, the woods meant there was lots of birdlife. Sometimes he watched them through his binoculars. He liked birds. He drove out into the countryside at the weekend to spot rare waders and geese. He remembered he had started watching birds – alone – after he no longer had his friend Peter to play football with as a child. After his accident.

Mr Edwards' mind flitted from birds to his pupils. He liked them too. They were nice kids. And a part of him regretted the start he'd made with them. Banning football: it was not a good way to endear himself to a hundred and twenty children. But it had to be done. For safety reasons. So there were no accidents.

As he gazed into the trees, he saw a movement. A flash of colour among the trees. Mr Edwards grabbed his binoculars. Was it the red throat of a swallow? Surely it was too late in the year for swallows? The leaves were coming off the trees; it was autumn. The swallows would have all migrated back to South Africa for the winter by now.

No. It wasn't a swallow; there were people in the woods!

Mr Edwards dashed to the door. Who were these people? He didn't know, but they were a threat to his children. And anyone who was a threat to the safety of his children had to be stopped. He hated to see children in danger. It was why he had become a head teacher: to look after children.

He ran through the staffroom, calling to other

teachers. As they came out of the school doors, to run across the playground, he had four teachers and a caretaker trailing behind him.

The children in the playground looked OK. Everyone seemed safe. But he was worried something was happening among the trees.

Mr Edwards entered the woods from behind

the back of the sheds. He worked his way through the undergrowth, dead leaves wet under his feet. The sound of the other teachers behind him.

And then he stopped.

At first he felt relieved. Relieved to see eight of his children playing football. And a part of him wanted to laugh and let them carry on, as he and the other teachers watched in surprise.

But he knew he had to show that he was in charge. That was his job, after all.

The first thing *Lily* knew about Mr Edwards discovering the Secret Football Club was when she played a perfect pass through to Maddie, but, instead of going on to score, Maddie stopped and let the ball roll away.

When Lily noticed Maddie staring in horror over her shoulder, she turned. And *there* she saw several teachers and dinner ladies standing breathless on the edge of the tennis court.

Nobody spoke for a few seconds.

And in that time Lily realized it was all over. Playing football. Their secret pitch. And all the consequences that would come of them breaking so many school rules.

Striking Out

Back in his office, Mr Edwards stood with the eight children who he had caught playing football.

What should he do with them? He had to be firm. He had told them that playing football at school was banned. If he didn't enforce the ban, he would lose everyone's respect.

And he regretted this, a small part of him wishing he hadn't banned football at all.

'You have all disobeyed two school rules,' Mr Edwards said in a low voice. 'One: that you are not allowed in the school woods. Two: that you are not allowed to play football.'

Mr Edwards looked out of the window at the trees. He wondered how long this had been going on. It was the first time he'd seen them playing. But he felt sure this was not the first time they had played.

And as he was staring at the trees, he noticed leaves falling, a red and orange shower as the wind blew. That was why he'd seen them: the trees were losing their leaves. Because it was autumn. They had been hidden until now. Mr Edwards almost smiled. But he had to be a head teacher. He had to appear firm.

'I will be telephoning all your parents and

asking them to come in so I can speak to them,' he said. 'This is a very serious matter.'

He looked at the children. Their faces were pale. At least two of them looked like they were going to cry.

After the children had gone, Mr Edwards sat at his desk and sighed. This whole business was troubling him deeply. It had brought back bad memories: memories he had tried to forget.

He closed his eyes and saw two clear images of his friend the day he was injured. One of him lying still after he had fallen and Mr Edwards thinking he was dead. The other of his friend running alongside

him down the wing, then playing the ball to his feet, for him to score.

It was only when Mrs Baker coughed that he saw her. How long had she been standing there?

'I knocked,' she said.

'I'm sorry,' Mr Edwards said quietly. 'I was miles away.'

'I wanted to speak to you,' Mrs Baker said, 'about Lily and her friends.'

Mr Edwards nodded. 'I know.'

And he gazed out of the window again. This was supposed to be a happy time: the school celebrating its centenary. Not a sad time. He wished his friend Peter was here. Maybe he would have a good idea how he could find a way of solving this problem.

Unbearable

Lily felt stupid putting on her fourteenth-century clothes for the school celebration. She didn't feel like celebrating anything – certainly nothing to do with school.

Any day now her mum and dad were going to get a call from Mr Edwards. All weekend she'd been trying to work out how to tell them.

So what if the TV news were coming to film them? And that Mr Edwards wanted everyone on their best behaviour – to show Kingsfolly Primary School to be the best school in the borough. Lily wasn't sure it was the best school. How could it be if they weren't allowed to play football?

At the school gates – with all the year groups mixed up – the school looked ridiculous. There were World War One soldiers talking to astronauts and Victorian beggars arguing with Vikings.

It just made Lily even madder. This whole anniversary was a joke. A farce.

Mrs Baker spoke to class before the celebrations began.

'You all look wonderful,' she said. 'The perfect fourteenth-century football team.'

Maddie looked up from picking at her dress.

'That is what you are, isn't it?' Mrs Baker asked.

'We might as well be,' Lily said, 'seeing as we've been banned too.' She saw Zack and Khal nodding opposite her.

'Well, I think you look great. But you need one more thing,' Mrs Baker said. And, out of her bag, she lifted a football. But it was not an ordinary football. It was painted. Blue and yellow and white. With words in black, written beautifully, saying KINGSFOLLY FC.

The class stared.

'Remember I told you about the fourteenth-century footballers.'

'The ones who were banned?' Khal interrupted.

'Yes. The ones who were banned. But who carried on playing.'

Lily smiled as Mrs Baker caught her eye.

'And that they played with highly decorated balls.'

'Yes,' Maddie said.

'Well, this is *your* ball. Just for the photographs, you understand. And the TV cameras.'

As the rest of the class nodded, fireworks went off in Lily's head: she'd had an idea.

In the playground each year group was asked to stand in their designated place.

The TV people had arrived, along with lots of

parents who had been invited to watch the celebrations, which were going out live on a morning news show.

Each year group staged a short re-enactment of their time in history.

The parents watched.

The cameras filmed.

Mr Edwards smiled: this was making the school look good. Like it was a nice school.

When it came to Year Six's turn, Lily was meant to start their play. The idea was that they should throw the ball around, to show how mob footballers dressed. And what their ball looked like.

The TV man behind the camera put his thumbs up, meaning they should start.

But Lily was not feeling right. She'd never been on television. The idea of millions of people watching her made her feel very nervous – and she knew she had something she needed to do.

So she sat down. On the ball.

'And what is it *you're* doing?' the TV interviewer said, looking slightly uneasy.

'We're fourteenth-century mob footballers,' Lily

said. 'But King Edwards had banned us from playing football. So we can't re-enact the game any more.'

'But you can pretend today, can't you?' asked the interviewer, smiling. 'It's not like football is banned at this school, is it? In the twenty-first century?'

And, for a second, Lily didn't know what to say.

Let's Play

After Lily had nodded her head in answer to the interviewer's question, deciding it was best not to say anything, the TV camera team turned to Mr Edwards, who was standing behind them.

'You're the head of this school, aren't you?' the interviewer asked. 'Mr Edwards, right?'

Mr Edwards nodded.

'And is football really banned?'

'It is,' he replied.

The interviewer turned to Lily. 'And how do you feel about that?'

'Sad,' Lily said.

'I'll bet,' the interviewer said. 'Mr Edwards, may we ask *why* football is banned at your school?'

'Because it is dangerous. And I do not want my children hurt.'

'But surely it's only football?'

'People can get hurt,' Mr Edwards said firmly.

The interviewer looked confused and she said, 'But people can get hurt crossing roads, opening doors. Surely it's no more dangerous than anything else.'

'We have no playing fields at this school,' Mr Edwards said. 'If we did, then it would be possible. But all we have is this small playground. And it is

up to me to protect everyone in the playground.
A playground that is shared by Years One to Six,
I should add. And I choose to offer that protection
by banning ball games.'

No one spoke for a few seconds.

Then another voice cut in. It was Oliver Sykes.
'You could play in the woods,' he said.

Lily stared at Oliver. Oliver the football hater –
suggesting they should be allowed to play football?
He smiled back at her. And Lily realized what he
was doing. He was helping because he thought
the football ban was wrong, even though he didn't
like football.

'The woods?' said the interviewer.

'The children have been playing in the woods,' Mr Edwards interrupted in a quiet voice. 'They made a pitch. To play in secret.'

'I have a great idea!' the TV interviewer said after a short pause. 'How about a game? In the woods. Teachers versus children. And if the teachers win, then football stays banned. And if the kids win, football is allowed.'

Some of the parents who had been eavesdropping cheered. Mr Edwards looked at the ground. As if he wanted it to open up and swallow him. Then he felt Mrs Baker's hand on his arm.

He looked at her. She was nodding, urging him to agree.

Mr Edwards turned to the children and shrugged. 'Very well,' he said, with a slight smile. 'Teachers versus children. The winner takes it all.'

Lily couldn't believe what had just gone on. Was this really going to happen? And the funny thing was, Mr Edwards actually sounded pleased at the idea.

Great Expectations

Six days later the woods were full. Full of children. Full of parents. And the TV people were there too: filming the challenge game of football that had excited the whole city.

All week the children of Kingsfolly Primary had talked about nothing else. Could a team of Year Sixes beat teachers at football?

They were about to find out.

The children lined up in their strongest formation:

                    Zack

    James   Maddie

        Lily   Batts

            Khal

Rebecca and Finn were substitutes.

On the teachers' team the notable players were Mr Luxton the games teacher in goal, Mrs Baker, in defence, and – up front – Mr Edwards himself with Mr Jones.

The TV interviewer had offered to referee the game, and, when she blew the whistle, a trio of pigeons took flight from the trees above the Secret Football Club's home ground.

The children started well. They knew the pitch. And they knew each other. Lily, James and Khal had the ball for the first minute, passing it in triangles, making the teachers run around in circles.

Lily could hear people laughing because they thought it looked so easy.

Secret FC's first chance came after two minutes:

Khal one-on-one with Mr Luxton in goal. But Khal, who was usually deadly one-on-one, scuffed the ball.

'What's up?' James asked. 'That was a sitter!'

Lily walked over to her team-mates. She wanted everyone to stay positive.

'It's the cameras,' Khal said. 'They're making me nervous.'

Lily and James looked over at the TV cameras. This game was going out on the local news that night. Suddenly Lily realized how strange this whole situation had become. The Secret Football Club was meant to be that: a *secret*. Now it was going to be on TV.

The next time Khal got the ball near goal, rather than shoot, he passed it to Lily. Lily was so surprised that she missed the ball, letting Mr Luxton pick it up and bowl it out to Mr Edwards.

Mr Edwards trapped the ball, turned and chipped it towards Zack's goal.

But Zack was looking at the TV camera too. Not the ball. And the first he knew about it was when it had bounced past him and Mr Edwards was jumping in the air, shouting, 'Goal!'

The teachers were winning one–nil. And Lily realized that there was a really good chance Secret FC would lose this game.

The Football Beast

At half-time it was still one–nil to the teachers. And James was losing his cool.

'This is rubbish. We're losing to the teachers. We're losing our right to play football. *And* it's all going to be on TV tonight. I'm off.'

Lily shook her head. 'Don't give up now.'

'Why not? This is embarrassing!'

Lily knew that if James left they had no chance. They needed six players who really cared about winning. She had to do something to make them gel as a team – so they could win this game.

'James,' Lily said. 'I want you and Maddie to go up front. Me and Khal will drop back and defend. You can score the goals for us!'

James looked at her, saying nothing. Lily wondered if he understood, or if he was about to disagree.

Then they heard Mr Edwards shouting for them to come back and play. And James surprised everybody.

'OK,' he said. 'I'll do it.'

The new team looked like this:

                    Zack

        Lily   Khal

                    Batts

        James   Maddie

Suddenly the game was very different. Secret FC
was on top. The teachers weren't getting a kick. It
was like the woods were on their side.

Two minutes into the second half Maddie passed
to James, who ran towards the goal. He looked to be
in a good position – with the hope of scoring.

Until Mr Edwards came lunging in to tackle
him, throwing his fifteen-stone frame at James's
six-stone body.

There was no way James could avoid the tackle. But James somehow managed to skip over their head teacher, clipping the ball over his tackle too.

He'd done it. Done the impossible.

And now he was one-on-one against Mr Luxton.

James struck the ball. Hard.

When it flew through the air it seemed to whistle, it was travelling so fast. So fast that no one saw it until it came back off a large oak tree and hit the teachers' keeper on the back of the head.

It was one all.

Lily leaped into the air. Her mind was going mad. Maybe they *could* win this. Maybe they *would* be able to play football.

They only needed one more goal.

She could feel herself grinning. She looked at all her team-mates. They were smiling too.

'COME ON!' Lily shouted. 'This is it. We're going to win.'

Captain Fantastic

Mr Edwards kicked off after the equalizer.

He looked cross. Or was he excited? Lily couldn't be sure.

She watched him tap the ball to Mrs Baker, who played it straight back to him. Then he started one of his runs. Beating player after player. Only Batts' firm tackle stopped him giving the teachers the lead again.

The game was end to end.

Mr Edwards was making attack after attack. He was the only teacher who could really play. After he nearly scored again, Batts hoofed the ball up the pitch. Just to get it out of the way of Mr Edwards.

But James was at the end of Batts's long kick. He controlled the ball perfectly, side-stepped one teacher and slammed the ball past Mr Luxton.

Two—one to the children. Lily couldn't believe it.

She ran up to James and hugged him. Followed by everyone else.

As they broke up, James looked at Lily. 'I'm sorry,' he said.

'What for?'

'For giving away the secret.'

You would have thought that, after that, things would go well. That the children would go on to win. That they'd be allowed to play football again.

But it didn't.

A minute later the teachers equalized. Mr Edwards again.

Two–two.

'He's good,' Maddie said breathlessly to Lily.

'I know,' Lily replied.

There was a minute to go.

James had passed a ball back to Lily. And Lily played it to Maddie. But Maddie stumbled and Secret FC lost the ball. To Mr Jones.

Mr Jones wasted no time and played the ball to Mr Edwards, who ran at the goal, knowing there was barely any time left. He sprinted past Khal, then past James, then Batts and Lily, leaving Zack running out of his goal to reach the ball before the head teacher could shoot.

But it was not to be. Mr Edwards reached the

ball and tapped it to the right of Zack. Zack fell to the ground, but could only watch Mr Edwards go past him on the left.

Then he heard him shout, 'Gooooooooaaaaaaaal!'

And it was. An easy tap-in. An open goal.

Three–two.

It was over.

Heroes

When the TV interviewer blew the final whistle,
Lily dropped to her knees and looked into the
wood, away from the TV cameras. She loved
this wood.

The thoughts in her mind were that she might
never be allowed here again. That she would have to
stop playing football forever.

Then she saw a hand reaching down to her.

Lily looked up. It was Mr Edwards.

She took his hand. 'Well played,' she said, trying
to be a good loser.

'Well played, you,' Mr Edwards said in a soft voice. Then he pointed to the TV camera. 'They want you and me to do an interview. Please will you come with me?'

Lily did not want to be interviewed for TV, but, because Mr Edwards had said please, she thought she should.

They walked together to the TV camera. It was only when they got there that Lily realized she was still holding Mr Edwards' hand.

'So, Lily,' the interviewer said in a cheerful voice, 'you lost the game fair and square. Are you going to give up your protest?'

Lily nodded. And at the same time Mr

Edwards spoke: 'Yes, she is going to give up her protests.'

Lily wondered what else the head teacher would say. That she was going to be punished too?

'. . . because I am in awe of her.'

The TV interviewer looked suddenly at Mr Edwards. 'Really? What's this?'

Mr Edwards turned to address the parents and children and teachers, as well as the TV crew.

'*Who* are you in awe of?' the interviewer asked.

'Of Lily,' Mr Edwards said. 'And her friends.' He cleared his throat. 'How long did it take them to clear this wood to make a football pitch here? Weeks, I suspect. How creative have they been to find a way of doing something they love? Very. I am in awe of them all.'

Nobody spoke. It was like they were waiting for the punch-line in a joke.

'From today, the school is going to invest in this football pitch. We are going to make it a little bit safer. And Lily and her friends are going to play on it as much as they like. As are the rest of the children at Kingsfolly Primary School.'

Lily stared at her friends. They were all grinning. She looked at Mrs Baker, who smiled back at her too.

'I was wrong to ban football.' Mr Edwards gazed into the trees, as if he was looking for ideas among the leaves. 'I was worried about danger and protecting the children. When I was young, a friend . . .' Mr Edwards stopped himself. 'But that's another story. What I have learned this week is that these children are special. They are talented and clever. Here, they've had a real knock: their favourite pastime taken away from them. And did they suffer? No. They thrived. They learned. They grew.'

Mr Edwards turned to Lily and Khal – and the rest of the Secret Football Club – and continued: 'I'm sorry, children. I was wrong. I'd like to be your team's number-one fan.'

Lily grinned. And then she had an idea. A great

idea. Mr Edwards was obviously very good at football. He could help them.

'How about you become our coach too?' she suggested.

Mr Edwards frowned. 'I don't know much about coaching football. I'm not sure . . .'

'You can play it, though, can't you?' said James, putting his arm around Lily. 'We'd love it if you would be our coach.'

And after a moment's thought, with all the parents and teachers and pupils watching him, Mr Edwards nodded.

'Yes,' he said. 'Yes, please.'

Tom is really pleased that he has been chosen to write a brand-new Pocket Money Puffin story, to celebrate Puffin's 70th birthday. Did you spot that each chapter is named after a Puffin book? If you like the sound of a title, why not see if you can find a copy of it in your local library or bookshop.

Thank Yous

When I visit schools I am always asked how a book comes about. Do I write it by hand? Who helps me make it as good as it can be? I hope this list of thank yous helps to explain.

The Secret Football Club was commissioned by Puffin, who wanted me to write a football story to help them celebrate their seventieth birthday. They asked me to write a book somewhere between 8,000 and 10,000 words long. I agreed and want to say thank you to Puffin for thinking of me for one of the books.

Before I wrote *The Secret Football Club* I read a book about mob football called *Uppies and Downies* by Hugh Hornby. It told me all I needed to know about the old forms of football – and much more. If you read a book to help you write a book, it's important to mention it and say thanks to the author too.

When I'm writing a book I always talk it through with my wife. She comes up with lots of good ideas and helps me make the right decisions. But *The Secret Football Club* was also important because it was the first book my daughter, who was five at the time, helped me to write. We talked about it on a car journey and I took lots of notes. (My wife was driving.) So I have lots to thank them both for. As well as their undying support for my wanting to be a writer.

Once I'd written the first draft my wife read it. She is always my first reader and spots lots of ways I can improve it. Then I ask a small group of friends to read it. My neighbour Nikki. A teacher in Basildon: Diane. And my agent, David. They gave me great feedback and, because of what they said, I cut out about fifteen pages where Kingsfolly Primary School play another school. Thank you to all of you for that.

Next, I showed it to my writing group. There were three writers in the group at the time: me; James Nash, a poet; and Sophie Hannah, a poet and crime novelist. They gave me lots of advice too. Thanks to them. I made more changes after they suggested the head teacher needed altering.

A week before I sent the book to Puffin, finished, I read it to my daughter. It is really helpful reading it to her, because she makes great comments and helps me see which bits are a bit boring and need jazzing up.

After all that, my publisher, Puffin, works its magic: magic it has been working for seventy years. My editor, Helen, helps make the story as good as possible. Then Wendy checks through the text for mistakes and inconsistencies. They help make this the book it is. Thank you to them too.

And I mustn't forget finally everyone else at Puffin who gets to work on it. The cover designers design covers. The publicity and marketing teams promote it. The sales team sell it to bookshops. Without them, no one would ever know about the book, so they are as important as any of the above people, who I'd like to thank one more time.

Thanks too to the bookshops and libraries who support my – and other Puffin – books. Their support really helps get my books to readers. It is much appreciated.

My final thank you goes to *you*, the reader. Without you, there would be no one to write for and so there'd be no books in the first place!

It all started with a Scarecrow.

Puffin is seventy years old.
Sounds ancient, doesn't it? But Puffin has never been
so lively. We're always on the lookout for the next big
idea, which is how it began all those years ago.

Penguin Books was a big idea from the mind of
a man called Allen Lane, who in 1935 invented
the quality paperback and changed the world.
**And from great Penguins, great Puffins grew,
changing the face of children's books forever.**

The first four Puffin Picture Books were hatched in 1940 and the
first Puffin story book featured a man with broomstick arms called
Worzel Gummidge. In 1967 Kaye Webb, Puffin Editor, started the
Puffin Club, promising to **'make children into readers'**.
She kept that promise and over 200,000 children became
devoted Puffineers through their quarterly instalments of
Puffin Post, which is now back for a new generation.

Many years from now, we hope you'll look back and
remember Puffin with a smile. **No matter what your age
or what you're into, there's a Puffin for everyone.**
The possibilities are endless, but one thing is for sure:
whether it's a picture book or a paperback, a sticker book
or a hardback, **if it's got that little Puffin
on it – it's bound to be good.**